OF MYRIAD PATHS

TO RESILIENCE, TENACITY AND HOPE

By SAAL BARAAN

Illustrated by Antonija Marinić

OF MYRIAD PATHS

TO RESILIENCE, TENACITY AND HOPE

Cover design by Nada Orlić

Interior Design and Book Layout by Ana Secivanovic

Publishing and Formatting Assistance by Kali Browne

ISBN: 978-1-7332708-0-9 eBook
ISBN: 978-1-7332708-1-6 Print Paperback
Library of Congress Control Number: 2019909200

For all inquiries, please contact the author at: XYZ Parenting LLC
2211 South Telegraph Road, #7346
Bloomfield Hills, MI 48302

Email: saalbaraan@gmail.com www.saalbaraan.com

Dedicated to all the "Wonder Women" in my life:

My mom, the poet, lyricist and vocalist who cheered me
on for every verse I formed since age six

My wife Samina for being the ever-loving,
powerful force beside me

My daughters Zoha and Aleesa for their ever-blessed
presence and joy they brought me

Introduction

I wrote these poems over the past 3 years. They have
undergone multiple revisions. The objective is to appeal
to the emotion and to the intellect. I wanted these poetic
themes to be supplanted with beautiful illustrations which
would add another dimension to the poems.

Each of these poems represents fictitious characters that
are based on real-life stories. Readers should be able to
relate to some of these stories. The identities have been
stripped and any connectivity to actual persons is purely
incidental and not intentional.

The stories are lifelong lessons and intended to make
us ponder solutions and encourage constructive action
individually or collectively.

The Background:

It started with seeing what we call 'difficult' cases,
whether in my clinic or in the nursing home. These
interactions would inevitably leave me exhausted, sad,
and wondering about potential solutions. It became
more intense as I started grappling with my own aging
parents and their issues. I began to feel helpless. I wrote
about these matters and sought some clarity with poems
and with illustrations. One topic followed another, and it
turned into twenty-one pieces and illustrations.

The stories are portraits of ordinary courageous people
with extraordinary resilience and tenacity and hope.

i

The Cover:

The picture on the cover appeals to my heart. A pair of autumn leaves hanging onto a branch with resilience, tenacity and hope, not unlike my parents in their 80s holding onto their faith, to their values, and to their hopes.

The leaves, like the arboreal branches all around, could have taken so many paths, and yet they are here. Likewise, once they leave, there will be many paths to follow.

I found the depiction of this theme through the picture to be powerful.

The Book:

This book is a collection of poetry and illustrations and it addresses the difficult issues of losses in myriad forms-loss of youth, memory, identity, privilege, security, mobility, employment, dignity and status just like the loss of leaves from autumn trees. Yet, there is a resilience in these characters. They hang on with hope and therein lies the learning for us.

Saal Baraan

Acknowledgements

My utmost gratitude to my wife Samina Bharwani, first for encouraging me to pick up my passion after a long hiatus, second for relieving me of household responsibilities which provided me with ample focused time to devote to my project, and lastly for her periodic guidance.

I am thankful for my daughters Zoha Bharwani and Aleesa Bharwani for sharing their views on the cover page and fonts and sharing with me their stories and ideas.

My gratitude to my brother Seraj Bharwani and my sisters Azizeh Moosa and Nadia Ladak for their belief in my poetry. I thank my sister-in-law Rozmin Bharwani for her encouragement.

Thanks to my friend Jazmin Jamal for challenging me to come up with matching verses to the lines that she would WhatsApp me from time to time.

Special thanks to Illustrator Antonija Marinić for her illustrations in this book of poems. She was dedicated to the project and gave justice to my poems. She helped me achieve my dream of crossing the mediums and create this book of poetry with illustrations.

Special thanks to Poet Laurie Filipelli for her guidance and mentoring and for opening my eyes to the wealth of North American poetry.

I thank especially my coworkers-doctors, nurses and administrative assistants-for their incredible support at my workplace. Sandra Hodges, Cynthia Hansen, Sharon Jones, Allison, Christina and Tracy. Thank you all!

My very special gratitude to my Chief Dr. Souheil Gebara and Chair Dr. Brian Berman for providing me with the environment to thrive and succeed and find my passion too.

My deepest gratitude to my mother Noorbano Bharwani and my father Shamsuddin Bharwani for providing a rich environment of poetic literature from my early life. My mom, herself a poet, recited poetry in Sanskrit, Hindi and Gujerati. I learned of Indian mystic and poet Bhagat Kabir through her rendition of his poetry. Kabir wrote poetry in the fifteenth century.

It is through my mom and dad that I learned so much of Sufi poetry literature. Between the two of them, they had memorized over a hundred of the ginans, a genre of eastern meditative poetry.

Sufi traditions and literature have produced poetry in the form of ginans, granths, ghazals, manaqib and qaseeda. Together, these exposed me to verses in Urdu, Hindi, Gujerati, Punjabi, Siraiki, Sindhi, Turkish, and Persian languages.

I am grateful to my high school teacher Mr. Abbas who would push me often to write a verse worthy of respect from my poet ancestors. I failed often.

The ancestors like Rumi, Meer, Ghalib, Iqbal, Faiz,
Blake and Milton being proud of me—I am not so sure.

Later, Wordsworth and Longfellow took my fancy.
Finally, Frost, Dickinson, Milton, Poe and Pound grabbed
my admiration.

I must thank the two poets who inspired me to combine
the medium of poetry with illustrations—William Blake
and Khalil Gibran.

This technique of combining poems with illustrations
engages multiple senses to experience poetry more fully
in my opinion. I believe in Horace's ut pictura poesis,
"as is painting so is poetry."

I should end by claiming that we are surrounded
with poetry.

For those of us with faith, we are indebted to the world
literature of scriptures—8600 verses of the Bible are
poetry, just like much of the Quran (Koran) is in rhymes.

For each one of us, there are myriad paths to poetic
experience.

Thank you for joining me in this journey.

Saal Baraan

Contents

Of Myriad Paths

Her home lies across Henderson port.

The ships here chase the sun inland

From east to west and back to east,

a pendulum in a grandfather clock.

Each turn portends finality, but

swings back to begin afresh.

No dock for her eyes, just passing boats,

sleepy giants floating away.

A dim candle on the water, her beacon.

She waits for none, all loved ones gone.

The ships stay far and recede farther,

her loss like a curtain pulled wide and wider,

her life an arrow that left a long while back

to the bow's relief, out of the archer's sight.

It is easy to move closer to closure.

This untapped beauty, an unmet vigor

was tied back in Savannah, Georgia.

August hot afternoon, her intolerable gown

Craving for wind, blue bells and lilies,

cool shower, lemonade, wet feet in the pond.

The grey and faded wedding picture

adorns the corner of a spartan dresser.

As a child, holding her father's hand,

she walked the prairies, dreamt of beaches.

Hand-in-hand by the riverside then,

canoe ride and a soft kiss under the shade

of Sycamore trees, where her husband speaks,

of beaches, rivers, and cool breeze.

The river has shared many such dreams

carried away to the ocean in tides.

Where the babies cry their fate away

she lived alone for ninety seasons,

her husband lost with bass and perch,

the turning tide of fate. Where are her kids?

One taken an infant, one lost to war,

the paths were many but for the fear,

like an innocent child, she submitted,

waltzing when spirited were her heels,

long horseback rides when her heart desired

autumn leaves, few, tenacious and hopeful,

dreading the currents will sweep them far.

Was it ever hers, her so-called dream?

Was she right in holding onto it?

Of myriad paths, she chose the one to this port,

Like autumn's leaves, she shows resilience.

Dreams of Sleep

Miriam dreams of the sleep

She lost, the day he fell

Now a cup of tea, a reverie

Unpaid work that love demands

The love she can't recall

"Wiwam," he calls out

She goes to him, a bee

Emptying her belly

Drip by drip, draining

Corpse of a spouse, skeleton

Laconic–not by choice

Drools when she feeds him

How can a clot so small–

8mm–make an infant of a man?

Should love be so demanding?

To take zest out of our lives

Reciprocal tenacity, him and her

Who's more tenacious between us

Does the winner gets to sleep well?

8 mm

"Life – 120 days,

Five laps a minute,

No slowing down – until now...."

A temptation, a sweet spot

Let me rest in a tiny bend

A respite, a hideout, shhh!

Let the manic rush pass by

But more join me soon

A party soon begins

Revolt, rebel, relish

Red glow of delight

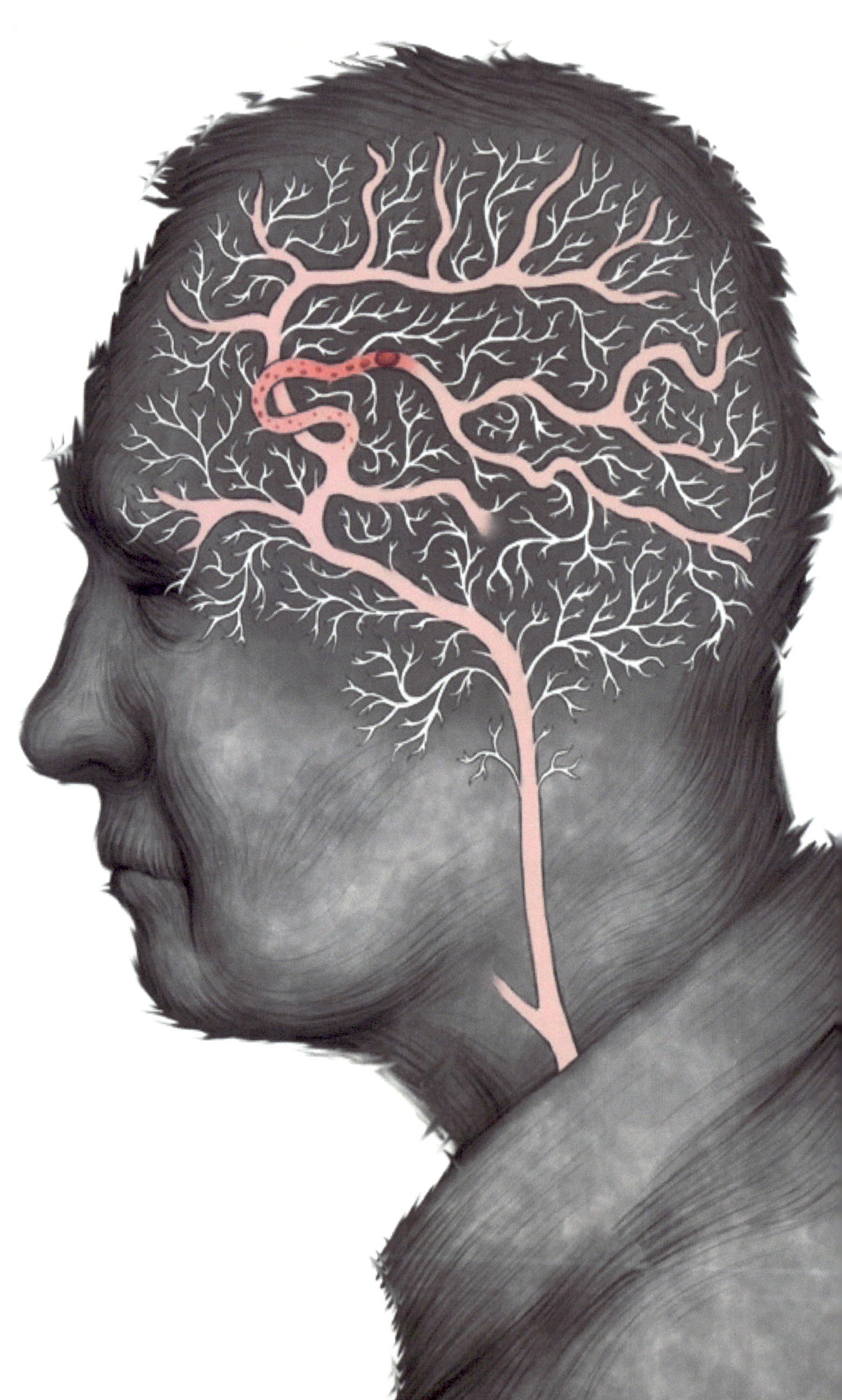

No fast pace in this corner

mini-Mardi Gras procession

8 mm long and 2 mm wide

We block the main artery

Miriam became 'Wiwam'

A twisted body, calling

From a twisted mouth.

Her name changes thus

How a clot so tiny

Locks one in for life!

Stroke! they call it,

A stroke of bad luck

66 Miles to Pain

Two half souls don't make a whole

Chasm between sanity and oblivion

The town has providers of pain relief

But we hide in the trailer park in pain

Choose relief to numb the soul

Or a pain that crushes the body

An ATV tumbled and ripped open his leg

Healthy truck driver turns disabled

A bartending wife left her job

To help her mate heal, but it costs.

Trading hope and work for pain and fear

Docs with scripts, dealers with treats

All promising instant relief and bliss

The docs lose licenses, dealers thrive

PAIN CONTROL
OPIATES
METHADONE Rx
NALOXONE Rx
ADDICTION Rx

The man grieves when the wife ODs,

She lives, they run away from it all

66 miles away from temptation

Clean sober life, again we will begin

Not one misstep to be swept away

We'll go to town with all the will

Say no to dealers near ATMs

Bag the groceries, bare necessities

Any pain? No; Pain relief? No, No

Steal the eyes from old acquaintances

Pick up naloxone, keep the opiates at bay

Quick, in the car, shack, safe retreat

66 miles is all the distance there is

between the numbness and the pain

Orange

*T*his is for you!

Out of her magic box of colorful pencils,

Orange she picks out.

She draws a tiny orange on a scrap of paper.

I look at the precious scrap and wonder.

My role in her life is writing scripts –

Scripts that make her bowels move

And take away some pain perhaps, some.

For the bladder, she calls her mom for tube in–

Drip, drip, drip, –and tube out, every 4 hours!

A 7-year-old in pull-ups, she chases her friends

In her wheelchair. With smiles, she goes on.

Friends from the church bus that fateful night,

Now running around, their feet on the ground.

Wheelchair as her legs, she tries to blend in

Cell phones and ringing sounds agonize her.

The sight of her sister texting only terrifies her.

Half-writ message on a broken, bloodied screen.

-Car Driver killed upon impact, tumbling my bus.

Police won't say more. She wished they would.

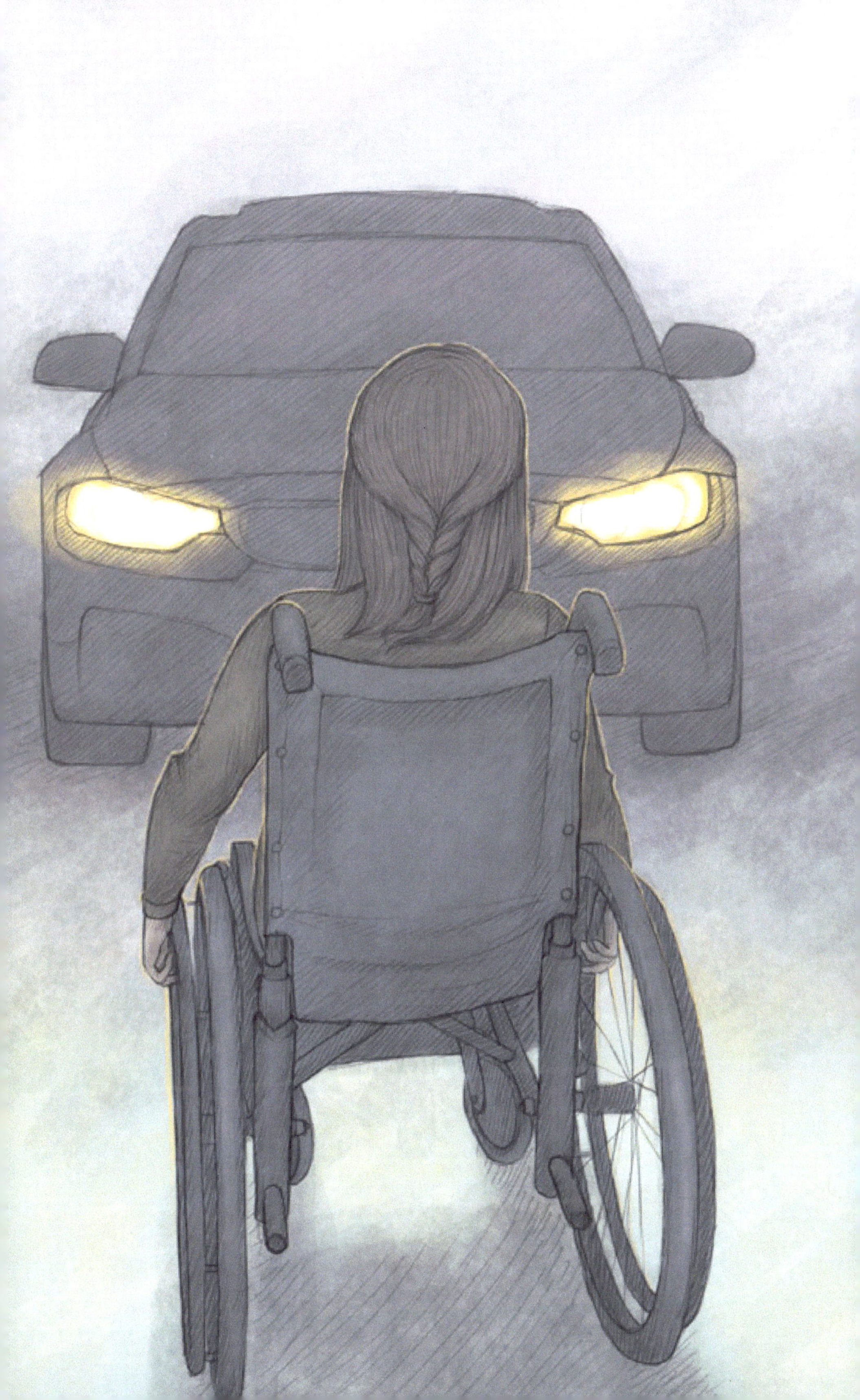

In fury she rams her wheelchair into the wall.

-*Leave me alone! Go away, you all!*

-*You promised me I will walk in a year, Daddy!*

-*Ants are running up and down my legs, Mommy.*

-*Watch out! Orange, fiery lights ahead.*

A bad dream that's all. Try to sleep!

-*I was the last they pulled out from under.*

-*How could a small car wreck a bus?*

-*The reverend says it was God's work.*

-*The Devil must be the phone then.*

Hills to Conquer

Thirty-four, single and worry free

I have mastered the art of the ski

Haven't I proved my mettle yet?

Why this angst within the chest?

Watch out for the scary face

The lines of 50 and 60 degrees

Breakneck speed down the slope

Two peaks to slide down between

Single mastectomy, double mastectomy

Choices are rough looking from above

I rip my line and up twenty feet in the air

Two more there and down into the chute

Thirty seconds and in the bottom

Surgery would be a lot longer

Duct cell carcinoma, left breast

Left me reeling since the news

Perfect BMI, my frame of steel

Athletic, vegan, sculptured body

Double mastectomy, single mastectomy

How will I ski this slope again?

Will my breast nurse a baby?

Will my body ever feel feminine?

Watch out now, the final edge

The cleavage that I'll never see

Double mastectomy, single mastectomy

I will make up my mind soon

I will conquer this evil descent

I will not hurtle into the rocks

Though I see the exposed ice

And this terrain is unforgiving

I will maneuver the death trap

Expansive powder waits below

The blow will be softened

The recovery should be swift

I am resolute, I will conquer

This hill is my witness, I will prevail

Bipolar's Wife

Tonight, I go to bed, another day gone

When I wake next to my husband,

When his eyes open, will he be there?

Awake and vigilant or a spirit downtrodden

His posture straight or his gait lumbering

My eyes strain from watchful wait

His choice of words will bring the tiding

I'll be ever watchful in my surfing

Plunging breakers or soft spillers

Sunny day brings me hope

Dreary day is a fence-walk

Losses and gains, flowering or cowering

Sunshine with a chance of fog or rain

Two selves, doubling songs and sorrows

Twice the giggles or the gut-wrenching sobs

Breakfast in bed, or a total abandonment

Bottomless hope and merciless fright

My bright tenor, poor husband

One day in tune, the following, out

Play the waltz, I'll dance tonight

If you lead me

Catatonia – The Third Response

Prying neighbor prowls daily

Concerned friends drop by

Self-portrait, still painting

Motion held in a trance

Is he a man or a mannequin?

Monk in deep meditation

Object permanently frozen

Tortoise when threatened

I'm Woodstock standing still

Wax doll in a museum

Place me in a different spot

A locked door with keys lost

I hear all, and I see all

My peace is in utter stillness

I am free as freedom can be

I hide while you are exposed

Forgotten in any company

Hear the deals the women make

I know the tales the men spin

Curtains fallen around me

Fed on time, bathed on time

Daily toils are not for me,

I am hiding, to keep away

The pain that swallows me

No fright or flight for me

Mundane matters not for me

Abstract matters are beyond

Light or dark, I can sense too

-Cars passing, people walking by

-Dogs barking, birds chirping

-My wife's kisses, Rugby's barks

-My granddaughter Mia's squeals

Rugby's paws tickle me

He wants to play fetch

Nurse draws the curtains

Tablets I must swallow next

She'll turn the TV on for me

she'll speak her mind to me

Mia will now pull my legs

I'll respond as total mute

Dusting and cleaning starts

Chandeliers first, mirrors next

Precious vases in the end

And a tad more perhaps

Dressing and changing me

Face shaved, back sores covered

Put me away back in my place

A body blended with furniture

Professional Beggar

Fear me why? I am not aggressive

Just need some coins if you drop by

I will keep you at my arm's length, will not follow

I will stay away from your car unless you call

I am a professional beggar, I do it for a living

I don't care about the weather, I know it's cold

Minus 40 or 50 is all the same to my senses

I have my handwritten plaques to draw attention

To get some sympathy, you know what I mean

Business tactics, and it works on some

Seeing me out in the freezing cold

Bundled up and with shabby belongings

Some cars stop at this busy intersection

I get my spare change and they get my nods

HAVE
MERCY
PLEASE
NDOM
T OF
NDNESS
HAVE
GRE
D

I suppose it's a fair exchange if you ask me

Some curious folks humor me with queries

Are you homeless? Do you use a shelter place?

No, I am not, and yes, I do, for sleep!

Do you get free food? Why do you beg?

I do, but I buy my own food sometimes too

Are you a veteran? A war hero? Destitute?

No, I am none of these, but for you I can make up stories

Why aren't you working? You look able-bodied

I have worked thirty-eight jobs in the past twenty-four years

My mania or depression always get the better of me

I don't last long in any conventional task, fired

I work my hours now, show up most days,

My terms, my hours, flexible work schedule

This junction is my fortune and my office

Come rain or shine I stand in this corner quiet

The city has been generous, but some remain unkind

Call me junkie as they throw coins at me

Glances of contempt, my cross to bear

You don't do drugs, you ask me?

No, not me, but I enjoy beer Friday night.

Why don't you get your mental illness fixed?

It's not cheap, no money to pay the counseling fees

When I make enough money here, one day I will!

Till then I'll hold on to this place tight,

For other beggars, this is a coveted site

Now if you excuse me it's a prime time

I am a professional beggar, I do it for a living

Mine or Yours

Patriotic act you had thought

Done in honor of your nation

The risk you took upon yourself

In hopes to be a living legend

A proud bearer of mighty hope

Like so many others before you

Your anger seeps away in ruins

Hate words emblazoned on my door

My shop ablaze in orange flames

Your blushed face beams with pride

The graffiti dancing in your eyes

You surrendered when caught

The deed done, you submitted

You smirked at me and then I asked,

'This is my country, where is yours?'

These should have been your words

The thought never crossed your mind

That I could be a citizen of this land

Could you within and I without

Reconcile through our racist guile?

May we come around one day

And cheer to the land we share!

Lest we burn the seeds of fear

Weeds of terror will grow again

Mere Mortals

Sixteen helicopters rest, ready for combat

Three donkeys climbing stone rail

Drops of blood mark the mountain trail

I hope my donkey knows the way

I wish to live long to tell this tale

The care is so near my dear

Baby will be fine, you hear

They're warm right by the stove

Four at home, this baby's the fear

Lips are dry, please one more sip

Felt a rip down at the valley's dip

No one says how far the center is

No doctor, quick, a nurse, a drip!

The jolts of the cart and searing pain

It could take days, but I must strain

The snowy wind howls, gusts of rain

Lightheaded, dizzy I feel young again

Kicking the dust under my bare feet

Collecting rocks, roaming the street

Hair shortened to disguise as a boy

Then I am twelve, a girl and retreat

In four walls, from the men's clan

Soon married off to an elderly man

Four births since then, I never ran

Now woman in labor on a donkey

Birthing lady gone, war took her man

Sun is down, again it starts to rain

woman stooped, in stress and strain

Sack on the fatigued mammal's back

Days on this path, my will in the drain

Seven Apaches zooming by and I crane

Scoop me up, I am your battle spoil`

I see it, I see it, the doctor is near

We are losing her, fever is too high

The donkey was slow, our luck was dry

Mother and baby rest in peace tonight

No Place to Hide

A reality show where we hide,

Hide to survive! Be invisible

A warrant for a million people

Threatens lives of many folks

Eyes of all colors following me

My head, a bouquet of symbols

Foremost a Symbol of Terrorism,

Welfare abuse, of refugee status

Of free tuition, of alien intrusion

Of evading taxes and of stealing jobs

Of diluting the culture and tradition

Of committing crimes, of living illegally

I *am a citizen*; You shouldn't be!

My brother serves in the Navy; Invaders!

I pay taxes. I work two jobs; Lies!

I paid tuition; You're on food stamps!

You're misinformed, Remove your scarf!

I am not repressed. It is my choice

My culture, my unique ID, my voice

It means no harm to anyone around

Go back to where you came from!

A man's hateful eyes pierce me

A pocketknife flashes open

He hops to the seat beside me

The passengers gasp, now aghast

Nobody moves, frozen in fear

The train stops, not my station

I jump out, panic clutches me

I do not look back, the streets are dark

Walking fast, I clasp my head scarf

My hair is covered, but there is more to me

Blind are the open eyes that follow me

Restitution

She wants to meet, and I don't know why

Barred for five years by a hundred-foot fence

Not a word I have to speak even now

Yet bound to her by that fateful night

Me, behind the wheel of Jack's red pickup

Outside a rowdy bar her son and his friends

In a Chevy sedan at 2 a.m.

We met on Hwy 24 at 150 miles per hour

Lies, all lies, clear skies and motion

No sandstorm churning, no blizzard's sway

No fog to cover me this time

Memory fails, only flashes of a bonfire,

Charred turkey fumes, metal on metal

Wrists behind my back, Aunt Leila forgot

To turn the oven off, the alarm rings loud,

Blazing sirens, fireworks of blue light

A million shards of glass, sting on my cheek–

The kiss of concrete against my sticky face

My blood alcohol made no sense to me

Wouldn't she want me dead? A son for a son

It is only fair–when one cries, another's eyes fill

The mothers wept that night

for their sons lost–one to time, another to death

Tonight, she'll take me to her son's room

Banner flag Maize and Blue-Wolverines

His selfies with his golden retriever

Posing in front of that shiny blue Chevy

Barred for five years, fenced by a hundred bars

Feelings no longer prisoned deep within

Final Escape

Rowing across the snaky river Charles

Motorbiking under the shiny distant stars

Balancing the tease of wind and surfing waves

A misstep on the road and amidst the cars!

I wake up with a startling, achy breast

To the aide's pounding on my chest

Breathe, cough– get it out, all of it!

Dreams that always end in nightmares

If this was sleep let me wake up straight

I am dancing in Le Caveau de la Huchette

Fine aroma of a French Haute cuisine

Feet light in my Louboutins for a date

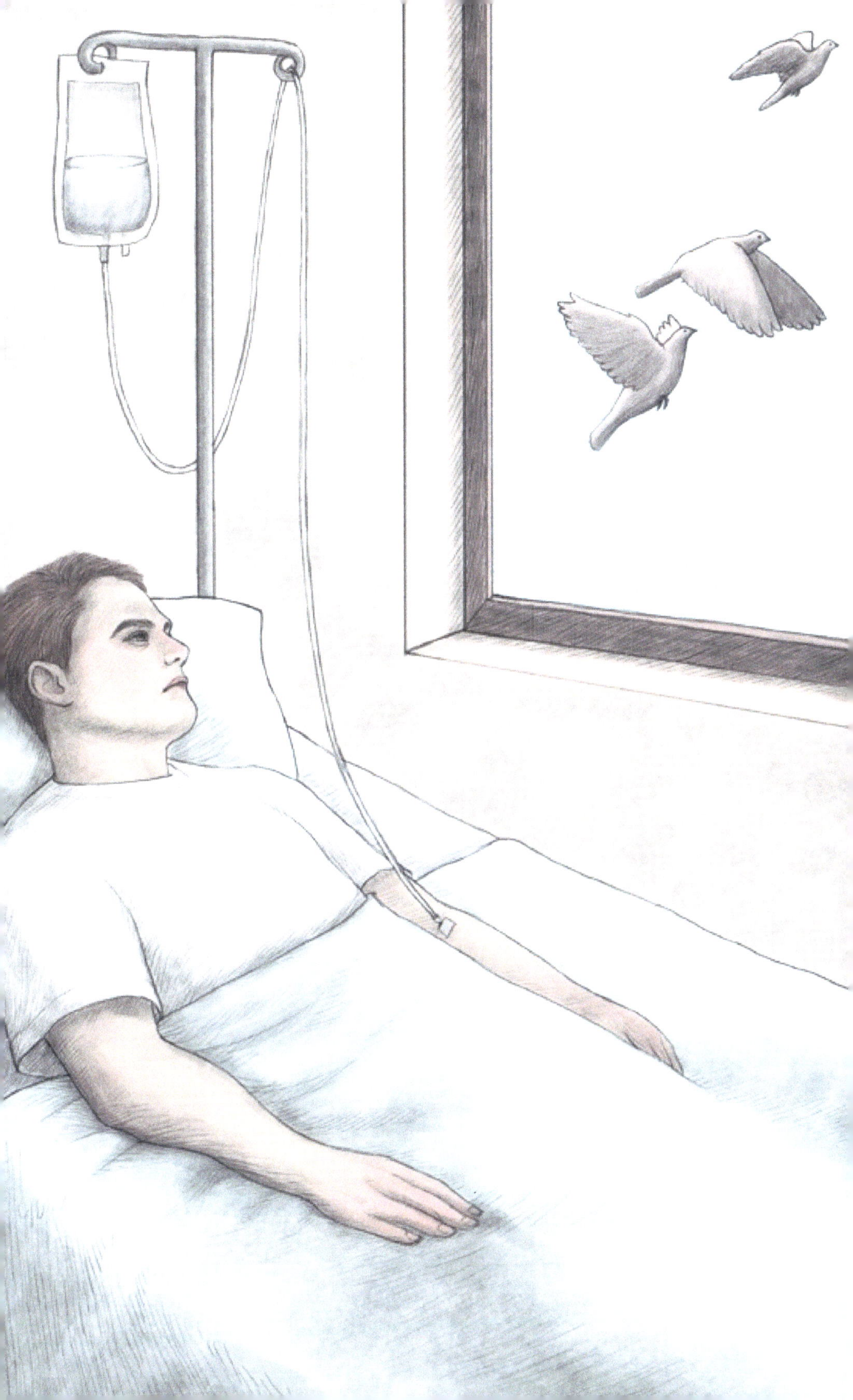

A medic's eyes caught mine open, sad

C7 fracture they said, prognosis bad

Stretcher, CT, surgery, rehab, home

Hit-and-run that left me flat and afraid

Medic arrives with weary eyes on sight

Cough, more cough, throat feels tight

Boys and girls, let's carry him out

Ambulance, Oxygen tank, ICU, right?

Sleep takes me to Avenue Montaigne

I am lifting a glass to taste champagne

My fiancé in her gorgeous gown smiles

Nightmare has ended, pain remains

Vial shatters in familiar jittery ride

Oxycodone, fast, now the other side

Pounding on the chest begins anew

Suction, nebs, epi, resuscitate, dead

The sleep-wake cycle in circles spin

The pain is constant from chin to shin

Find me an escape hatch, now to unpin

Tired of submission to dream and grin

There might still be a final option

Needs deft and craft in its execution

A failsafe escape when all else fails

The Prince has lost the will to go on

Thoughts of death, a longing to cease

One painful breath after another, forever

The escape, an absolution to my existence

Just another realm? Take me there in stealth

Can I dance again for all the money I have?

Thousand therapies and I still don't feel brave

IV Potassium please, grant me eternal sleep

Peace of body, mind and soul is what I crave

Healing in distress

Apple brandy to set bone from the blows

Slice of beef to dice tumor in the nose

Magic when quinine booted fever out

When opiates in sugar blurred the gout

A bushel of corn for the doc for cleaning a wound

A handmade quilt for delivering a newborn

Lawn work for the relief received with castor oil

Clothes mended for getting Epsom for the boil

 I, the doctor, am one of the family

Here my pay is in cash or in service

I see the patients—rich and poor alike

Contract binds me with my charges

I hold floppy hands, and I wait

Till they shake mine with vigor

I am drowsy and groggy, at my limit

When the baby perks up and smiles

I feverishly move on, case after case

Till the Typhus fever epidemic breaks

My hands toil till the man's can till again

My balms calm the deep burns of fire

I know little of what lies beneath the skin

I have one treatment for ten maladies

People look at me with hope and with awe,

My bag in possession of magical powers

For pain, analgesia, for surgery, anesthesia

For fever, antipyretic, for vomiting, antiemetic,

For every infection, a targeted antibiotic,

For prevention, myriads of vaccinations,

Ten prescriptions for every malady,

Yet the patient's insurance dictates

Rejections, denials, prior authorization

My hands are forced into what I write

I must see thirty patients a day or else

My fixed salary takes a cut for the worse

My patient and I report to the payers

Suspicion for me when once there was trust

I face a challenge while internet holds credence

I've lost my years and my debts take their toll

My hours are long, and my calls oft repeat

I document forever, I defend my plans of care

I see no real value in the toils I endure

Burnouts and suicides, I see my peers face

Rich MBAs and MHAs have MDs on a leash

Which patient do I see? what money do I make?

Doctors are tenacious, doctors are resilient

But the pressures have led many to leave

Of myriad paths I chose the one of suffering

My demeanor betrays diminishing powers

A Few More Credits

The battery is dead and so is the car

The fridge is a picturesque empty bar

But for my favorite intimate apparel

The wardrobe is an ugly dated bazaar

Neighbors wonder why I never leave my place

Onscreen like emoji keeping ever-smiley face

I flirt, text, seduce, I'm a hot webcam girl

Nerdy Mikes and Monkey Daves jam my space

Men buy credits, steadying the flow of cash

The walk to the nail job is a long painful dash

Makeup comes cheap, a friend does my hair

Camera zooms on my body, my bed in a flash

With credits to spare, you can meet me virtual

Chat and strip in private, the stream is perpetual

The days turn to nights and nights to empty days

My webcam crosses oceans but wait is my ritual

Your pleasure is my business, you are running low

Watch out for your credits Joe they're coming too slow

You love my accent? Awww! Do you like what you see?

The camera hides the walls where the molds grow

Genuine Joe you fell into my space somehow

Intrigued me, disturbed me, I don't know how

Whole of me to see and you zoomed on my face

Called it heavenly, captivating, mesmerizing, WOW!

Against my reason I revealed my real name

Beyond judgement, beyond reprieve, and far beyond shame

You touched my soul, made me feel like a Queen

And I acted like a slut like I do without blame

Show me your face Joe, let me hear your voice

I swoon over your texts, your words I rejoice

The shabby room and the man-boys on the cam

I need them for the credits, not by my choice

I feel exposed here, sitting, clothed in lace

My cheeks burn as I feel your eyes embrace

Faceless, ageless, voiceless texts behind my cam

Tell me your real name and show me your face

Belle is my cam name; you can call me Blagorodna

Noble woman it means, but I scavenge in Macedonia

Used, abused, now you make me dream, it's too late

I cannot be a muse, or a queen or a lovely ballerina

And yet your praises seem real, Mr. Genuine Joe

You rise above the rest, but my cash is running low

I can fake, pretend, I can be your slutty cam girl

You're the fish in my net, so enjoy Belle's show

Trafficked in Moldova, escaped from Belarus train

From sleazy Johns and romantic Robs I refrain

Waiting behind my web cam in Skopje's shanty parts

For a few more credits Joe, won't you come again?

Headphones with Earbuds

*I*t started with the search for headphones

The picture clear in his mind, the name elusive

How could he ask his wife what he was looking for?

How could he ask his daughter?

Name, what was the name again? Let's not panic

Listening device, but there are thousands of them,

the one you put in your ears, not hearing aids,

not stereo phones, earpiece, no, has cords attached,

sound-free, phonic, no, not headset—the charade goes on,

Merry-go-round in his mind, endless agitation

Cruel is the word he can think of, cruel it is,

Internet—answer to my prayers now. Safari, I remember

Quick search, what? Private listening? Duh!

Secret listening, spyware, sound capture, bla bla blah!

Ear plugs, earmuff, recorder-plugin-music, NO!

Its nauseating, crazy, disturbing, earpieces,

Images, Goddammit, look at images, Headsets,

There, that one, item #4144, headphones,

Headphones with ear buds. Yes, YES!

For goodness sake headphones, headphones,

Relief seeping through his demeanor,

How the hell can one forget headphones?

Hang on to me, my mind, please don't let go!

The Gash That Wakes Me Up

*T*wenty-five years and the scar still wakes me up

First the screams and then the muffled sighs

It talks to me of whispers amidst loud gun shots,

Of secret hiding places and of trusts betrayed

Of losses large and small, and of legacies made

My right foot rests in a deep, achy sleep

To people, it is just a scar, a childhood folly

No, it's a story unfolding far away in Tibet

One million people killed out of six million strong

Someone's uncle, somebody's mother, taken

My brother, my niece, and my neighbor's son too

Murdered, maimed and thrown with the rest

A sixteen-year-old, I earned the rebels' raves

Raised raucous, yelled and made waves

Captured one night and thrown into a prison

Isolation, deprivation, total abandon

Over the barbed-wire fence I jumped one night

Landed onto the razor-strewn ground below

Piercing pain, enough to freeze my heart

To stop me in my tracks across the ground

A perimeter patrol thrusts his bayonet blade

My drive to flee was stronger than my pains

But he got me deep within, nonetheless

Life seeping through my bloodied foot, I ran

But fell on the shards of broken glass

Then onto the bed of rocks I tripped again

My screams muffled by their cruel laughter

The guards thought they got me at last

A cacophony, a set designed for the escapee

Floodlights and search guards now on my tail

My blood on the rocks, blazing a trail

I was the proverbial wounded animal

but led by flight response, not by fight

Sight of train tracks brought spirits to heights

Lying low, cowering from the glaring lights

Prayed for a fast train but slow enough to climb

A train did slow, and my heart leaped fast

My pulse had no room to go top speed

A chance I cannot miss (my shooter sure won't)

Blood rushed into my injured legs, energized

Eyeing the gap between the first and the second cars

I hobbled and waddled, hopped onto the metal bars

I pressed the X, the door opened, I collapsed

Feverish and in sepsis, I dreamt of freedom

Patched up in a hospital near a river bend

A Nepali doctor cared for me for weeks on end

Major surgery and twenty days in a comatose state

Beyond the border, soon back to life, to freedom

I died many a death in the intensive care ward

But for my deeds, Tibet, I can never return

Blacklisted, exiled, I miss my family so

My consolation is this gash in my foot

It's a memory, a story that I weaved

Age of Madness

Welcome to the madness

In bliss, blister or rage

In silk, satin or wants

Blessed and the cursed

In foggy days and crystal nights,

Chaos is washed by clear dreams

Longings for silence when lucid,

When screams guard the hallways

Darkness soils the windows thus

Time is narrow and the space wide

The luck running out each passing day

Every moment saved; a moment lived

I do not trust them; none save only one

She comes here often and gives me a name

Smiling she says who she once was to me,

I believe her sometimes, it makes her smile

I wish I could say that I remember

A pile of albums and pictures she brings

Places I've known before, faraway lands,

Palm trees and coconut drinks, poolside tables,

Amtrak station, Delta terminal, desert and camel

Me sporting a big fish, proud in fishing gear,

Pontoon in the backdrop, people gathered,

A boy grinning, seagulls circling above

It's there, all there, proof and evidence

Near bassinet, a stroller, a necklace of daisies

Little girl in a pink headband, no front teeth

Black-and-white dress, glaring sun, glass

Four candles and a boy in a comical hat

Blue-and-pink balloons, smell of chlorine,

Floating sheet music, faded ink,

Sloshing across a soaking carpet,

Drowned teddy bear, moldy smell

Graduation cap and gown,

The grill I fired up, a family feast

Aboard a Royal Caribbean cruise liner

Holding on to her floppy straw hat

Waving her other arm at me,

Me in my trucker cap and shorts posing

Tanned skin and salt-and-peppery chest

Welcome to the madness, the undermined age

You may be wise, or you may be a fool even now

You are now the living and the lived, holding on

Every moment saved is a moment haunted

Alone while a noisy bunch gathers nearby,

I ask about the lady and am told there were many

One arrives and smiles and she could be the one

the same, I cannot tell—What does she want from me?

Milton

The curtain falls but there is no applause

The monitor goes blank without a glitch

The unplugged toy flashes for seconds

The lizard sheds its tail.

Tylor smiles, Sarah giggles, the world feels alive

If only Milton could be alive again!

Milton was alive once, a bustling town

Cars and buses were loud; people laughed

No dope on the streets, minds were sound

Mona laughs. Rick joins in, Terri flirts with Jerry

Bottles of booze, smoke, drown the despair

Raises specter of hope, until the hangover

Heydays are gone, Milton's lost paradise

Cheers to the ghost town of Milton!

Liquor bar the only hub of fun and life

HOTEL
LIQUOR

That was the last laughter for Mona

The burial was quick and cheap.

Four people stood, cigarettes in hands, impatient

Backhoe kept digging, the rain kept pace

Rick said Mona was special, not strong

Booze-another round till words retire

Tylor slept and Sarah tried to mourn

Her mother's prom night picture stared at her

Imposing, direct gaze, round brown eyes,

Curly shoulder-length hair, frilly knee-high dress

Mother you almost made it.

Three daughters you raised since Daddy left

K-MART loved you, but it left too

And so, did your dreams

Booze was easy, smokers all around

You lost your love for living

I will be stronger than you Momma

I will keep my job, not marry young

Let Johnny try to woo me

I will be your pride, pride of Milton

Mona died at fifty-two, her mother at forty-eight

Sara looked perfect in her prom dress

That girl will make something of herself

Say the Milton folks again with hope

Strong enough to resist the flaws of Milton

Milton died while people lay asleep

Internal bleed—slowly hemorrhaging

People were leaving, stores kept closing

Poor souls left behind for a miracle

Sarah dances away like a breeze

Autumn Leaves

The place is somewhere in between

You lost the luster but not the sheen

You're not too young nor I very old

It was dust after all that sold for gold

Hurtling to older, slowly but surely

Slighted by youth, blindsided by heft

Two tied a knot and now in a bind

One, part body, the other, half mind

There is none "this too shall pass"

Both of us, no doubt, will pass

There is no 'for better or for worse'

That is the way-better and worse,

The spirit breaks, the ego loses,

The urge to die, and end, bemuses

The sight looks, demurs, sighs!

Sound? Hollows of long goodbyes!

The loved ones far, the nurse close by

Going, going down, can't see up high

Comic tragedy that no one ever dodged

Beginnings vary, ends just the same

Like worn out clothes, spirit washed out

In lieu of zeal, the senses are engorged

Autumn leaves we are, lets fall in grace

leave the stem that fails to embrace,

No, autumn leaves stand up with might

Never leave the stem without a fight